MG   4.5/2.0

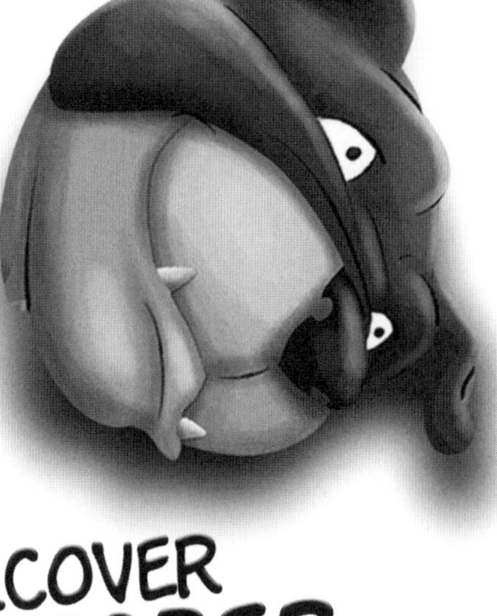

THE UNDERCOVER CHEERLEADER

STONE ARCH BOOKS

a capstone imprint

SNOOPS, INC. IS PUBLISHED BY
STONE ARCH BOOKS, A CAPSTONE IMPRINT
1710 ROE CREST DRIVE
NORTH MANKATO, MINNESOTA 56003
WWW.MYCAPSTONE.COM

Library of Congress Cataloging-in-Publication Data
Names: Terrell, Brandon, 1978– author. | Epelbaum, Mariano, 1975– illustrator. |
Terrell, Brandon, 1978– Snoops, Inc.
Title: The undercover cheerleader / by Brandon Terrell ; illustrated by Mariano Epelbaum.
Description: North Mankato, Minnesota : Stone Arch Books, a Capstone imprint,
[2018] | Series: Snoops, Inc.
Identifiers: LCCN 2017002466 (print) | LCCN 2017005201 (ebook) |
ISBN 9781496550613 (library binding) | ISBN 9781496550637 (paperback) |
ISBN 9781496550651 (eBook PDF)
Subjects: LCSH: Cheerleading—Juvenile fiction. | African American girls—Juvenile fiction. |
Hispanic American boys—Juvenile fiction. | Sabotage—Juvenile fiction. |
Best friends—Juvenile fiction. | Detective and mystery stories. |
CYAC: Mystery and detective stories. | Cheerleading—Fiction. |
African Americans—Fiction. | Hispanic Americans—Fiction. | Best friends—Fiction. |
Friendship—Fiction. | GSAFD: Mystery fiction. | LCGFT: Detective and mystery fiction.
Classification: LCC PZ7.T273 Ul 2018 (print) | LCC PZ7.T273 (ebook) |
DDC 813.6 [Fic]—dc23
LC record available at https://lccn.loc.gov/2017002466
Design elements: Shutterstock: In-Finity, loftystyle, veronchick84

BY BRANDON TERRELL

**ILLUSTRATED BY
MARIANO EPELBAUM**

EDITED BY: AARON SAUTTER
BOOK DESIGN BY: TED WILLIAMS
PRODUCTION BY: KATHY MCCOLLEY

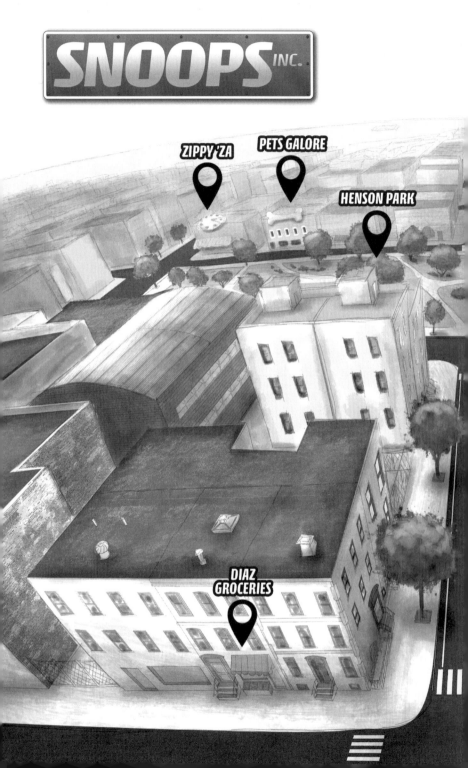

CHAPTER 1

A UNIQUE SNAPSHOT

The man in the trench coat strolled into the
dead-end alley without a care in the world. It was
the middle of the afternoon in the city. There wasn't
a cloud in the sky. The man in the coat looked a
little suspicious. But he was playing it cool. He
didn't act like he had thousands of dollars of stolen
watches hidden in his coat.

The alley was the perfect spot to meet. There were no windows, just brick walls on three sides and a single dumpster against one wall. The man sipped coffee from a foam cup. As he passed the dumpster, he lifted the lid and tossed in the nearly empty cup. He set the lid back down, careful not to slam it, just as he heard footsteps behind him.

A second man, this one skinny and more nervous, had entered the alley. His hair was ruffled. Sweat stains bloomed under the armpits of his button-down shirt. He carried a briefcase and strode quickly over to the first man.

"Do you have them?" the second man asked. His eyes flicked over to the alley entrance, as if expecting someone to appear.

The first man smiled. "Relax," he said. "Everything's here. Is that the money?" He nodded at the briefcase.

"Yeah."

"Then it's a pleasure doing business with you."

The two men were unaware that they were being watched — from the unlikeliest of places.

Inside the pitch-black dumpster, which was thankfully almost empty, sat two very patient young detectives. Twelve-year-old Jaden Williams removed his baseball cap and wiped the dregs of the man's coffee from it. "Phew, that was a close call," he whispered. "Dude almost saw us when he threw away his . . ." he sniffed his hat, "mocha latte."

Keisha Turner, a year older than Jaden, pressed a finger to her lips to shush him.

Jaden ignored her. "What?" he whispered, his voice nasally. "This is the stinkiest stakeout ever. We smell like old takeout food and rotten burps."

Keisha pressed her eye to a tiny hole the kid detectives had drilled into the side of the dumpster. The two men making their illegal deal were about ten feet away.

"How are we supposed to see anything stuck in here?" Jaden asked.

"Watch and learn." Keisha grabbed a white cardboard pizza box from Zippy 'Za. It was a little crumpled, with dried out flakes of crusty cheese stuck on one side. Hayden, Jaden's twin sister, had shown her this trick, and it had blown her mind.

Keisha held up the piece of cardboard — the side not stained with grease and tomato sauce — in front of the hole. A pinprick of light gleamed onto the cardboard. She slowly backed the pizza box up. The light grew brighter. Miraculously, an upside-down image began to appear on it!

"Whoa," Jaden whispered.

"It's like a pinhole camera," Keisha said, remembering what Hayden had told her. "The light from outside comes in through the tiny hole, like the lens of a camera."

"Good thing it's a sunny day outside," Jaden replied.

Keisha adjusted the pizza box. The image showed the two men outside. They were in the process of exchanging the briefcase of money for the stolen watches. "Quick," she instructed Jaden. "Snap a photo."

Jaden used his phone to take a picture of the image on the pizza box. Despite the low quality of the image, the men's faces were plainly visible. He tapped the *send* button on his phone and waited.

* * *

Three blocks away, fourteen-year-old Carlos Diaz sat perched on a bus stop bench. Traffic zipped past on the street in front of him. On the opposite sidewalk, two police officers stood next to their squad car, sipping coffee and chatting.

"We got 'em!" Hayden Williams, who sat on the bench beside Carlos, piped up. One of her favorite grape suckers was wedged in her mouth. She held out an old electronic tablet. On the screen was the grainy photo Jaden had sent her.

Carlos leapt off the bench. "Awesome!" he exclaimed. "Keisha and Jaden really came through in the clutch." Then he quickly strode across the street with Hayden at his heels. From his back pocket, he withdrew a folded piece of paper.

"Excuse me," Carlos said, waving at the two police officers and flashing his widest smile.

"Everything okay, kid?" one officer asked.

Carlos unfolded the paper and held it out. It was a printout of a wanted poster from the police department's website. On it was the man who was selling stolen watches in the alley.

Hayden held up the tablet next to Carlos' printout. The resemblance was uncanny.

"Looking for this guy?" Carlos asked.

"That's Barney Marsh, the jewelry store robber," the second cop said.

"Where'd you get that photo?" the first cop asked, putting down his coffee.

* * *

In the alley, the two men were finishing their deal. The first man double-checked the briefcase to make sure the money was in it while the other placed the stolen watches in a bag.

As they did, a loud screech erupted from the end of the alley. A police cruiser came to a stop, blocking the entrance completely.

"Oh no!" the second man shouted. He dropped the watches and thrust his arms into the sky.

The first man froze. Two officers entered the alley, followed by a pair of kids.

"Long time, no see — Barney Marsh," the first officer said.

The thief placed the briefcase on the ground and raised his hands. The two officers slapped handcuffs on both men.

"It's okay now," Carlos said loudly. "You can come out!"

WHAM!

Jaden shouldered open the dumpster lid, and it banged against the brick wall. He took a deep breath, as if he'd been holding his breath. "Finally!" he said.

"The pinhole camera worked," Hayden said, bumping fists with Keisha.

"Like a charm," Keisha said.

The two stunned thieves stood with jaws open as the officers led them to the waiting cruiser.

"Congratulations," Carlos said to them.

"You've just been busted . . ." Keisha added.

"by the super-stinky . . ." Jaden said, wrinkling his nose.

"Snoops, Incorporated!" Hayden finished.

CHAPTER 2

WE'VE GOT SPIRIT,

YES WE DO . . .

"Over here! I'm open!"

Keisha waved her hand in the air and Hayden fired a bounce pass to her. She quickly put up an arcing jump shot just out of the reach of Jaden's outstretched arms. The basketball rattled on the rim, and then fell through the hoop.

"Count it!" Keisha gloated.

"Yeah, yeah," Jaden grumbled. "Lucky shot."

Keisha and Hayden slapped a high-five while Carlos and Jaden took the ball on offense.

The young detectives were enjoying a pick-up game of b-ball in the gym at Fleischman Middle School. The gym's old hardwood floors and brick walls bounced sound in every direction. A set of wooden bleachers sat against one side of the gym. At its top was a balcony area.

"Come on, man, let's do this." Jaden spun his baseball cap backward like he was getting serious. Keisha could still see the coffee stain on it from the stakeout in the dumpster.

In fact, she could still smell the 'old takeout food and rotten burps' on herself. She'd even showered twice to try to get rid of the smell. Still . . . garbage.

Oh well, she thought, *you do what it takes to bust a criminal.*

Jaden put up a hook shot, but the ball bounced off the rim and sailed across the gym. Keisha easily beat Carlos to the ball. She snatched it up and dribbled past him. She glided by Jaden and finished the play with an easy lay-up shot.

"Nice moves!" Hayden shouted.

Footsteps began to swell through the gym. Keisha turned and saw a mass of girls entering like soldiers marching onto a battlefield. She rolled her eyes.

"Here comes the Spirit Squad," she said.

"*Rah-rah*," Hayden added sarcastically.

The girls swarming the gym floor were all dressed alike: a Fleischman Bulldogs sweater and a skirt to match. Their hair was pulled back in tight ponytails, making it hard to tell who was who.

Except the girl leading the charge.

Keisha knew exactly who that was.

Frankie Dixon walked with her chin up and her arms clasped behind her back. She was the captain of the Spirit Squad. At one time, Keisha and Frankie had been best friends. But Keisha's friendship with the opinionated, snobbish Spirit Squader wasn't the same as when they were kids. At least, not since The Fallout.

The Spirit Squad filed over to where the Snoops were playing basketball.

"Spirit Squad has gym time now," she said matter-of-factly. "You all have to leave."

"Great to see you, too," Keisha said.

"Our regional Cheer Bonanza competition is right around the corner, and we need to practice," Frankie explained. "We take this *very* seriously."

"You are quite athletic," a girl with a narrow face and blonde hair said to Keisha. Her mouth was tight, her expression no-nonsense. It didn't even seem like her lips moved as she spoke.

"Uh . . . thanks?" Keisha said. She didn't recognize the blonde girl.

"Nadia," the girl said. "Nadia Korlov. I'm new here. Have you thought of joining Spirit Squad?" she asked. "You would be a perfect fit."

Keisha looked at Frankie and said, "Yeah, I doubt that." She snatched up the basketball. "Come on, guys. Let's get outta here."

As they brushed past the Spirit Squad, a shorter girl with dark hair and gold-star earrings snickered. "Does anyone else smell that? Something stinks," she said, prompting giggles from the rest of the girls.

"Good one, Amelia," another girl whispered.

Keisha looked at Frankie, hoping her ex-bestie would say something, *anything*, in her defense. Frankie stayed silent.

Keisha could feel hot tears begin to form in the corner of her eyes. She lowered her head, tucked the basketball under one arm, and strode quickly across the gym. As she neared the door, she heard Frankie say, "Everyone take their positions. We've got a lot of work to do."

Keisha hurried out of the gym, fighting to keep her emotions in check. Insults and bullying were nothing to get worked up about. She was tough and had thick skin.

But Frankie used to stand up for her, used to have her back. Now, however . . .

* * *

After a fitful night of sleep, Keisha awoke to a new day. She took yet another shower, hoping the scalding hot water would finally wash away the foul-smelling stakeout.

With her hair rolled up in a thick towel and wearing a fluffy white robe, she left the steamy bathroom to get ready for school.

"Keisha, honey?" her mom called out from the apartment's living room.

"Yeah?"

"Can you come here a second? Someone's here to see you."

"If it's Carlos, tell him he's early," Keisha replied. "We're all supposed to meet at Snoops HQ in the basement before we walk to school."

"It's . . . not Carlos."

Puzzled, Keisha pulled her robe tight around her and walked down the narrow hall to the apartment's cluttered living room.

Standing next to her mother was the last person she expected to see — Frankie Dixon.

"Keisha," Frankie said. "I need your help."

CHAPTER 3

A NOT-SO-CHEERFUL WARNING

"Keisha?" Her mom snapped her fingers in front of Keisha's stunned face. "Sweetie?"

Keisha couldn't move. Frankie Dixon was standing in her living room. She hadn't been inside the Turners' apartment since . . . well, a long time.

"My help?" Keisha finally asked.

"Yeah," Frankie said. "I need Snoops, Inc. . . ." She trailed off, glancing toward Keisha's mom.

Keisha's mom had slipped away to the kitchen, where she was making her daughter's cold lunch. She didn't *seem* to be paying attention, but parents almost always were. "Well . . . I'd like to talk to you guys," Frankie finished cryptically.

"Hold up," Keisha said. "Gimme a minute, and we'll meet up with the crew."

She dressed quickly. For some reason, she felt uncomfortable leaving her mom and Frankie alone together. After Keisha grabbed her backpack and said goodbye to her mom, the two girls rode the building's rickety elevator to the basement.

"Keisha, what took you so long?" Jaden called as she walked into the storage area. The basement was lined with rows of chain-link fence storage units. Boxes and bins filled many of them. Carlos had converted an empty unit into Snoops HQ. It had a desk and chair, an old desktop computer, and a file cabinet.

"Sorry," Keisha said as she walked into their makeshift office. Frankie entered behind her. "I have a client."

"Frankie?" Jaden leapt to his feet like he'd been hit by electricity. He had a crazy crush on Frankie for some reason and always had.

Carlos stood near the file cabinet. "What's up?" he asked with a puzzled look on his face.

"Guys, I think Snoops, Incorporated may have a new case," Keisha said.

Carlos went directly into detective mode. "Give us the details," he said.

"I'd rather just show you," Frankie said. "Can we swing by my apartment before school starts?"

Hayden checked her watch. "If we leave now, we should have time."

"All right," Carlos said. "Let's roll out."

* * *

Frankie Dixon lived in a high-rise complex about five blocks from the Snoops' building. It was sleek and made of glass. A revolving front door led to a large lobby. Henderson, the doorman, greeted Frankie formally. "Back so soon, Ms. Dixon?" the elderly doorman asked.

"I forgot a book for school. You know me, I'm always forgetting something," Frankie fibbed easily, a fake smile plastered on her face. She continued to the elevators.

Keisha was both amazed and uncomfortable. Frankie and her parents had moved to this building shortly after The Fallout. Her dad's business, Dixon Dental, had struck it big-time, and their little apartment by Fleischman Middle School no longer cut it. Keisha had never been to Frankie's new home.

The elevator was made of glass. "This place is ridiculous," Jaden said as they rode smoothly up to the penthouse. His baseball cap was stowed in his backpack; he was trying to look his best for Frankie.

The elevator dinged, and the doors opened to a suite that made Keisha's jaw drop. It was beyond anything she'd ever seen before. It looked nothing like the small apartment where she and Frankie once made pillow forts and had sleepovers when they were younger.

"Last night, I invited the Spirit Squad over," Frankie explained as she led them into the apartment. She waved a hand toward a huge flat-screen TV hanging on the living room wall. "We hung out, ate popcorn, and watched footage from last year's Cheer Bonanza."

A set of glass French doors were open at the far end of the living room. Frankie walked to them. "This is Daddy's office. Totally off-limits. He's out of town at a dental conference . . . thankfully. Or else he'd have seen this."

She opened the doors dramatically. The office was a sea of dark, polished wood. Bookcases brimming over with books and trinkets, framed photos, and diplomas lined the walls. An immense desk with a metal sculpture of a tooth sat in the middle of the room.

It all looked normal. Except . . .

A table had been set up near the window. On it were the broken pieces of what, as far as Keisha could tell, was once a statue of something. The scene reminded Keisha of the cheesy monster movies her dad enjoyed. He loved watching giant lizards tromping through cities, crushing skyscrapers beneath big lizard feet.

"What is — uh, *was* — this?" Keisha asked.

"The model for Daddy's new building," Frankie explained. "His company is about to tear down that ugly old Kent Tower to build the new Dixon Dental Orthodontic Center. It's going to renew that whole neighborhood." She held up two pieces of the model, including the top of the building. A small statue of a tooth was perched atop it.

"This door is always closed when Daddy is gone," Frankie continued. "This morning, I found it cracked open. I peeked in and saw that the model was ruined."

"Did you tell your mom?" Hayden asked.

"No way," Frankie replied. "Daddy's office is strictly off-limits. If either of my parents found out someone was in here, I'm in big trouble."

"It looks like they left a note," Carlos said. He pointed to the table, where a slip of white paper

had been taped. Letters had been crudely cut out of magazines and pasted on the paper.

The note read: FRANKIE BEWARE.

"Whoa," Jaden said. "Whoever did this means business."

"Why are they threatening you?" Carlos asked. "Did you do something to upset anyone?"

"Of course not," Frankie said. "I'm the captain of the Spirit Squad. But I work hard to make sure everyone is included and has fun."

Yeah, right, Keisha thought, struggling to hide the sarcastic smirk that came to her lips. Instead, she took out her phone and focused on snapping photos of the crime scene.

"And nothing else was stolen or ruined when the Spirit Squad girls were here?" Carlos asked.

Frankie shook her head. "No. We were in the living room, like, the whole night." She looked down and grunted. "Ugh. This place is filthy."

The carpeted floor at her feet was sprinkled with bits of sand and grit. Some flakes of reddish mud were mixed in with it.

"Wait," Hayden said. She quickly slipped a plastic bag from her backpack and knelt on the floor near Frankie's feet.

"What are you doing?" Frankie wrinkled her nose in disgust.

"Everything's a clue until it's not," Keisha said. They watched as Hayden picked up bits of gravel and red mud and placed them in the bag.

A glimmer of light under the table caught Keisha's attention. "What's that?" she muttered. She knelt beside Hayden, reached over with another bag, and plucked the item off the floor.

"A diamond earring?" she said as the girls stood back up.

"Whoa," Carlos said. "That looks expensive."

"It is." Frankie leaned in close to inspect the earring in Keisha's hand. "It's not mine, but I can tell that it's a Francois Guion original design. The only place that sells them is Gold-Karat Jewelers in the Burlington Mall."

"Do you remember any of the girls wearing a pair last night?" Hayden asked.

"No," Frankie said, shaking her head.

Keisha passed the clues off to Hayden for safekeeping. She didn't like holding on to such an expensive piece of jewelry.

Jaden, who'd wandered back into the living room, called out, "There's more dirt out here!"

The group left the office. Jaden pointed to the floor near the huge TV. "More sand and dirt. It must have been on one of the girls' shoes."

"So it's definitely a major clue," Hayden said.

"Will you help me?" Frankie asked. "I need to know who did this. The Cheer Bonanza is next week. If someone on my team is angry, then we'll never be able to work together and win. Plus, Daddy's going to be so mad when he gets home and sees his hard work destroyed."

Carlos nodded. "Of course we'll help," he said. "Solving mysteries is what we do best." He thought for a moment and then added, "If the culprit is on the Spirit Squad, then we should really focus our attention there. You should have someone near you in case they act on their threat."

"The best way to do that is to probably have someone with Frankie at all times," Hayden said.

Jaden opened his mouth to volunteer, but Carlos cut him off. "Maybe we should even have someone join the Spirit Squad to keep a close eye on the rest of the team."

A cold feeling suddenly blossomed in Keisha's stomach. She knew where this was headed. Carlos and Hayden both looked in her direction.

"Oh no," she said, shaking her head. "Look somewhere else, dude."

"You're our best chance, Keisha," Carlos said. "What do you say?"

Keisha looked at Frankie. Her face, usually screwed up in disgust or smugness, was now filled with desperation. They'd been friends once, and Keisha had always told herself that she was the bigger person. If she refused to help Frankie now, that moral high ground would vanish.

"All right, fine," she said grudgingly. "I'll do it."

Relief washed over Frankie's face. "Yay!" she said. "Welcome to the Spirit Squad, Keisha!"

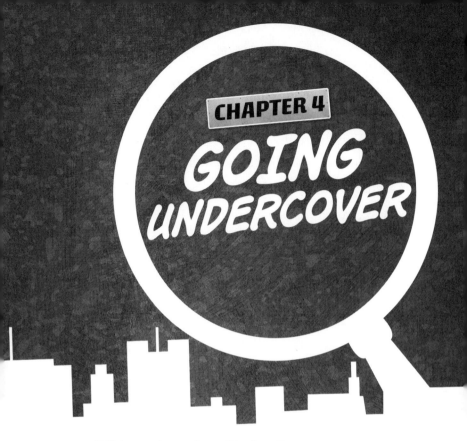

CHAPTER 4

GOING UNDERCOVER

"This . . . is . . . humiliating."

Keisha stood in front of a full-length mirror in the girl's locker room. It was after school, and she was now wearing the same ridiculous Bulldogs cheerleader uniform as the rest of the team.

Keisha hated how she looked, and wished she could go back to hanging out in a dumpster again.

"You look fine," Frankie said. "Come on, let's get to the gym."

Many of the Spirit Squad girls were already in the gymnasium. A few were stretching while others rolled out large blue pads across the floor. Keisha spied Nadia Korlov sitting on a bleacher reading a magazine titled *Cheer For Today.*

Nadia's eyes flicked up and saw Keisha. She leaped nimbly to her feet, stowed her reading material, and jogged over to Keisha and Frankie. "I see you re-thought the offer to join," Nadia said.

"Uh, yeah," Keisha said, adjusting her skirt. "I needed a challenge."

"I'm happy you're here."

Keisha looked around at the rest of the girls. Many of them were eyeing her up and down, but none seemed too suspicious of her . . . yet. It appeared as if Frankie hadn't spilled the beans about the damage at her home to the other girls. That actually kind of surprised Keisha.

Two girls stood under one of the gym's basketball hoops, speaking quietly. Keisha knew their names — Stella Lyndon and Kate Nicholson — but had never really talked to them.

As she secretly glanced at the two girls, another came loudly bustling into the gym. "Sorry I'm late," she said.

A girl with a human head and a bulldog's body ran into the gym. She was wearing the school's mascot costume — a bulldog named Chomp. Frankie's dad had bought the costume for the school after Champ, their real bulldog mascot, had gone missing recently. Chomp's head was cradled under the girl's arm.

"I had to pick this up before practice," the girl said. In her other hand was a long white tube. It looked like one of those toy rocket launchers Jaden and Carlos played with when they were younger.

"Is that the T-shirt cannon, Iris?" one of the girls asked the girl in costume. Keisha bristled when she realized it was the girl who'd made fun of her smell previously. *Amelia Thornton,* she thought.

Iris nodded. "It's really gonna wow the judges. And it's so easy to use."

"We're going to fire confetti at the end of our routine," Frankie explained to Keisha.

"Who's this?" Iris nodded at Keisha.

Frankie opened her mouth to respond —

"Okay, girls," came the voice of an adult from behind them. It was Ms. Buchanan, the girls' gym teacher and the Spirit Squad coach. She was lean and muscular, with a stern face. "Line up."

The girls stood on the blue mats. Keisha lined up next to Frankie, gazing around to see how the others were standing — head up and arms back. Again, they reminded Keisha of soldiers.

Coach Buchanan came right over to them. "Who's the new girl?" she asked.

"This is my friend, Keisha," Frankie explained.

Friend? Keisha thought. *That's a stretch.*

"She wants to join," Frankie continued. "I know our Cheer Bonanza routine is locked down, but she should be okay learning from the sidelines for now."

Scanning the squad, Keisha saw Stella's eyes rolling in Kate's direction as Frankie spoke.

Ms. Buchanan nodded. "Okay, then," she said. "Welcome to the squad, Keisha."

"Thanks, uh, Coach," Keisha said.

"All right," Coach Buchanan stated, "Let's start with leg exercises."

For the next two hours, Keisha watched the team perform their routine over and over. It was tiring, even though she was just hanging out on the bleachers. She couldn't imagine having Iris' job, running around and tumbling while wearing the Chomp costume.

Each time, as the routine ended, Iris held up the T-shirt cannon to mimic firing confetti into the air. Even through the costume, Keisha could see Iris' chest heaving as she tried to catch her breath.

Through it all, she didn't see a single scared look or guilty glance in Frankie's direction.

Apparently, whoever had destroyed the model and left the threatening note at Frankie's home wasn't afraid of Keisha. And no one appeared to be wearing earrings that matched the one they found in Dr. Dixon's office. Keisha had hoped to come out of today with at least one solid lead, but . . . nothing.

Keisha watched as Amelia Thornton launched herself into a tough sequence of eight back handsprings in a row.

"This is gonna be tougher than I thought," Keisha muttered to herself.

* * *

"Whoa! Now there's something I never thought I'd see!" Jaden grabbed his phone and snapped a pic of Keisha in her Spirit Squad uniform.

"Gimme that." Keisha snatched the phone from Jaden's hand before he could pull it away and immediately deleted the image.

"Aww," Jaden said, disappointed.

She had texted Carlos on her way home and discovered the rest of the Snoops were hanging out down at Snoops HQ.

"Ugh," Keisha said. "This has to be the worst case ever."

"So your first practice went well?" Hayden asked around the grape sucker in her mouth. Agatha, a stray tabby cat who hung out at Snoops HQ, was curled up beside her.

"Just great," she answered sarcastically. The plastic bag containing the note to Frankie sat beside the desktop computer. She picked it up and examined it again. The letters were all random, cut perfectly from different magazines. The only letter that stood out was the glittery, bright pink F in the word Frankie.

"Say, we've got a new case," Carlos said. "If you want to take your mind off Frankie."

"It's at Al's Castle Arcade," Hayden added. "Right next to the food court at the mall."

"Yeah, right by the food court," Jaden said dreamily. "Now that's my kind of case."

Keisha shook her head. "I'm exhausted," she said. "I just wanna curl up and watch some TV."

"I don't blame you," Carlos said. "The Spirit Squad — and dealing with Frankie — is a lot of work." He stood and readied himself to leave.

"Don't worry, Keisha. I have faith that you'll break the case."

"Thanks," she said glumly.

"That's the spirit!" Jaden said, pretending to shake a pair of pom-poms in the air.

Keisha just rolled her eyes. She didn't have the energy to respond. Hayden did it for her. She slugged Jaden in the arm.

"Ow!" he barked, following Carlos out.

Hayden bumped fists with Keisha. "Rest up," she instructed. "Bye, Agatha!"

Keisha nodded and closed her eyes. It was just her and Agatha in the office all alone.

"Lucky cat," Keisha muttered to the sleeping Agatha. She felt like curling up in a ball and joining the lazy feline.

* * *

The following afternoon, Keisha arrived at the gym early. Nobody was there, and the place was eerily quiet.

"Hey there." Frankie had appeared at the door.

"Oh. Hey," Keisha said.

Frankie looked around to make sure they were alone. "Any leads on the case?"

Keisha shook her head. "Not yet. Whoever left the note and destroyed the model is acting like nothing happened."

The two sat in silence for a moment, unsure what to say. Conversation between them had once been easy. Now, not so much.

"Wanna try a lift?" Frankie asked.

"Sure."

The girls stood face to face in the middle of the gym.

"Okay," Frankie explained. "I'm what's called a flyer since I'm lighter and get lifted into the air easier. You'll be the base since you're stronger."

"So, wait," Keisha said. "You want me to lift you up?"

"Of course," Frankie said. "It's easy."

Frankie showed her step by step until they finally tried the action. Frankie leaped up, and Keisha caught her feet in both hands. Like a weightlifter, she pushed Frankie up over her head. Frankie stood straight, keeping her balance.

"You're a natural!" Frankie said as Keisha brought her down. "Let's try it again."

The second lift was easier. As they worked, Keisha began to think that maybe, after all their differences, the two girls could still be a pretty good team.

During the third lift, Keisha saw a flicker of movement. A shadow moved on the balcony above the bleachers. But she couldn't take her concentration off Frankie, who was still held high above her.

WHOOMP!

The sound echoed across the gym. A split second later, a rain of confetti blanketed both girls. Frankie screamed and wobbled. Keisha's muscles strained to hold her up.

She couldn't do it.

Like a falling tree, Frankie came crashing down to the gym's hardwood floor.

CHAPTER 5
A CANNON AND A CLUE

Frankie hit the wooden floor with a *THUD!* and a sharp cry of pain.

"Frankie!" Keisha swatted aside the cloud of floating confetti. She knelt beside her friend, who lay clutching her right ankle. "Are you okay?"

"Ow . . . it hurts," Frankie hissed. Her ankle was already beginning to swell.

Keisha cast her eyes to the bleachers, but the shadow she'd seen a moment ago had vanished. Still, that was the direction the confetti had come from, and she had to check it out.

"What happened?!" Stella was the first to enter the gym from the locker room. A look of confusion was spread on her face.

Kate followed at her heels. "O-M-G, Frankie," she said.

"Someone fired confetti at us," Keisha stated. "I tried not to drop . . ." She trailed off.

A few more girls soon filed into the gym. Some had their phones out, texting others on the team. Coach Buchanan was not there; neither was Nadia Korlov.

"Frankie? Oh no!" Amelia Thornton rushed into the gymnasium. Her cheeks were flushed, like she'd been running. "I just got a text. I hurried as quick as I could."

It was surprising how quickly the Spirit Squad girls rallied behind their fallen captain. Especially considering how much she bossed them around.

As the girls helped Frankie, Keisha said, "I'll be right back." She hurried up the bleachers. When she reached the top, she hopped over the railing to the balcony area beyond.

A stretch of cement ran the length of the bleachers. At one end was a set of descending stairs. Next to the stairs she found what she thought she'd find: the T-shirt cannon.

It was lying on the floor, discarded after firing confetti at Frankie and Keisha. A few bits of the colorful paper lay scattered around it. Keisha scanned the area for clues but saw nothing.

"Whoever did this fled down the stairs," she whispered to herself. She carefully stepped over the cannon and walked down the poorly-lit cement steps. There was an open door at the bottom.

On the floor beside it, Keisha found a clue.

A plastic card, like a credit card, was hidden in the shadows of the bottom step. Keisha knelt down next to it. Although she didn't have any of Hayden's evidence bags, she picked the card up off the floor.

The card was red and green, with an image of a subway train and the initials CTA. "A City Transportation Authority pass?" she muttered. "This is for the 'El' train." The pass had no name on it, just a magnetic strip on the back. She couldn't imagine any of the girls on the Spirit Squad needing to ride public transportation.

Keisha slipped the card into the waistband of her cheerleading uniform.

On the other side of the door, she found herself in a hallway next to the gymnasium. She rounded a corner and was back at the gym's main entrance.

By that time, Coach Buchanan had helped Frankie to the bleachers. The others still stood around, hands clasped behind their backs and unsure what to do.

"Your ankle is pretty swollen," Coach Buchanan said.

"Will I be able to compete at the Cheer Bonanza?" Frankie asked, her eyes red-rimmed and swollen with tears.

Coach Buchanan answered quietly, "Doubtful."

"What? No!" Frankie blurted out. She looked away, seething with anger, lips drawn tight.

"Someone took this out of the locker room when they shouldn't have," Iris informed them. She'd retrieved the T-shirt cannon and held it cradled in her arms. "It's my responsibility."

"Well," Frankie said bitterly, "Did *you* fire it at me then?"

"Of course not," Iris said, sounding offended.

"Why would anyone want to do that?" Coach Buchanan asked.

Keisha looked around at each of the girls in turn. Whoever had done it certainly didn't seem sorry that Frankie had been hurt.

Frankie turned to Keisha. "I want to go home," she said matter-of-factly. "Will you help me?"

Keisha looked to Coach Buchanan, who nodded. "That may be for the best," she said. "Keeping it iced and getting rest will help."

"Sure," Keisha said to Frankie. "Let's go."

"Good." Frankie stood up, tried to put weight on her right ankle, and grimaced.

"Here." Keisha slipped one of Frankie's arms over her shoulder and propped her up.

The two girls walked slowly toward the door. As they exited, Keisha heard Coach Buchanan say, "All right, let's get back to work everyone. Nadia, I'd like you up front with me. You can take Frankie's place for now."

Keisha could see the hurt in Frankie's eyes and moved a bit faster.

* * *

As the elevator doors whooshed open on the Dixons' penthouse apartment, Keisha's breath was again taken away by the size of it. She couldn't imagine how Frankie had gotten used to coming home to so much space every day.

Keisha led her injured companion to the couch. Frankie slid down into the cushions with a sigh. "That's more like it," Frankie said as if *she* was the one who'd carried Keisha the whole way.

"Let me get you some ice for your ankle, and I'll be on my way," Keisha said.

The kitchen had a refrigerator so large it could hold enough food to feed an army. Keisha searched the freezer until she found a cold pack for Frankie and brought it back to the living room.

"Prop your ankle up," Keisha instructed, placing a pillow on the coffee table. Frankie rested her swollen ankle on it. She winced as Keisha applied the cold pack.

"I had to get out of there," Frankie said, tilting her head back. "Everyone was staring at me. I can't believe someone did that."

Keisha stepped toward the door. She wanted to get back to Snoops HQ and tell the others about what happened, and about the clues she'd found.

As if on cue, her phone chirped. It was a text from Carlos.

SNOOP_DUDE1: BIG BREAK IN ARCADE CASE. JOIN US @ HQ?

"So your mom will be home soon?" Keisha asked Frankie. "'Cuz I gotta jet."

Frankie shrugged.

"Remember what Coach said," Keisha reminded her. "Get some rest and keep your ankle iced. Your mom will want to take you to the doctor."

She walked to the door and pressed the button for the elevator. *Come on, hurry up*, she thought as she watched the numbers on the display creep up.

"Keisha?" Frankie asked. "Will you . . . are you sure you can't, you know . . . hang out here with me for awhile?"

Keisha noticed something she hadn't seen in her old friend for a long time. Vulnerability. Compassion. Fright. She looked truly scared.

"Sure," she said, after a moment. "Just gotta send a quick text."

KT_CLUE: CAN'T. @ FRANKIE'S.
LONG STORY.

Then she walked over and sat down on the couch next to her injured ex-BFF.

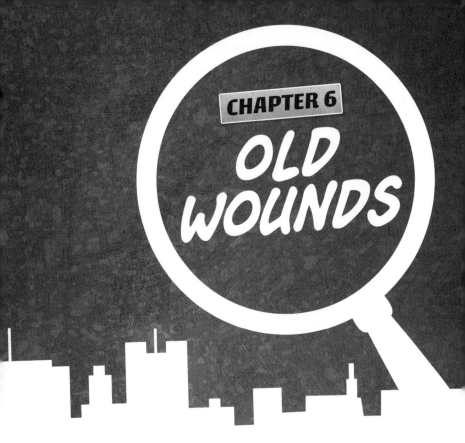

CHAPTER 6

OLD WOUNDS

"Do you remember when we slept in the tent in your living room?" Frankie giggled. "Your dad turned the TV to some nature show so we could pretend like we were looking at the stars."

"That was awesome," Keisha said. "We stayed up until, like, four in the morning."

"That was so fun."

The girls had been hanging at Frankie's for nearly an hour. Two cans of root beer and a bunch of snacks were strewn across the coffee table.

"Then there was the time we had to catch Mrs. Reuben's cat after it got loose," Keisha said. "We must have chased it around every floor of the building."

"And you leaped at it and fell into that potted plant instead," Frankie said.

Keisha laughed. "That was what? Like, a month before you . . ."

Moved. She'd wanted to say the word. The Dixons had lived in the same apartment building as Keisha. Then, in the blink of an eye, they'd abandoned their old place and moved . . . here.

And that had changed Frankie somehow. It made her feel more entitled, more important. And it had led the girls down the path to The Fallout.

A silence fell over the apartment. Keisha felt the mood shift and suddenly wanted to escape.

"Well," she said, standing. "It's been real, but I should probably go."

"Fine. I'm sure the *Snoops* are missing you," Frankie said sarcastically.

There it was. That tone. "Frankie, please don't start that again."

"Start *what* again?"

"You know," Keisha replied.

Frankie pretended to be shocked. "What do you mean? I was just saying your *real* friends are probably waiting for you. I saw the way you were looking at your phone, like you just couldn't get out of here fast enough."

"That's not fair," Keisha argued.

"It's cool," Frankie said. "You chose them over me. No worries."

Keisha tried to will herself not to bring up The Fallout. She tried to build a mental wall in her mind to keep the emotions back. But the dam broke, and they flowed free.

"You made me choose!" Keisha blurted out. "You said it was either you or them. That I had to decide who was more important. What kind of person makes her friend do that?"

"Keisha, we were BFFs — *B-F-Fs*," Frankie said. "Don't you get it? The second F? It stand for 'forever'."

"Yeah, well," Keisha waved her arms to acknowledge their surroundings, "apparently forever is a pretty short time in a place like this. After you moved here, you didn't make much of an effort to come back and see me."

Silence fell over them while Keisha jabbed at the elevator button, as if pressing it a dozen times would make it move faster. She didn't want to talk about it anymore. Didn't want to be around Frankie.

And she especially didn't want to think about what Frankie had done after The Fallout . . . when Keisha had chosen the Snoops over her. Frankie had made a collage of embarrassing photos of Keisha that the girls had taken over the years. Then she'd plastered them all over School Ties, the website for area schools, for everyone to see. She'd even added the word "TRAITOR" over the images.

"Maybe this is karma," Keisha said, turning back and nodding at Frankie's swollen ankle. "Maybe you deserve this."

"I . . . what?"

"You heard me," Keisha said softly as the elevator dinged. Keisha quickly stepped inside and pressed the first floor button. The doors closed, and the elevator whisked Keisha away in a whirlwind of anger and tears.

* * *

"Wait, say what? Someone fired a T-shirt cannon at you?!" Hayden blurted out.

Keisha looked around the crowded Fleischman hall to see if anyone had overheard. It was just past lunch, and Keisha was walking with Hayden and Jaden to their afternoon classes.

"Crazy," Hayden said, amazed. She plucked the sucker from her mouth and mimicked firing confetti out of it.

"And you think it was a Spirit Squad girl?" Jaden asked.

"I think so," Keisha said. "But I don't have a solid suspect. Any of the girls could have done it. Between that and what happened with Frankie, I'm not sure I what to think about this case."

"Is she okay?" Jaden looked concerned.

"She's the same old Frankie," Keisha said.

"But she'll miss Cheer Bonanza." Jaden shook his head. "Poor thing. I should send her some flowers."

As they reached one of the school's wide staircases, Carlos bounded down toward them.

"Carlos, you gotta hear this," Hayden said. "Tell him, Keisha."

Keisha filled him in on what had happened the day before. "So that's why you bailed on helping us at Al's Castle," Carlos said. "You were helping Frankie."

"We may have cracked the arcade case, by the way," Hayden said. "Carlos thinks Al's new employee is rigging games to lose and pocketing the extra cash."

"We're gonna stake it out after school," Jaden said, excited. "Maybe get a Juicy Smoothius and a CinnaRoll." He licked his lips, adding dreamily, "I can already taste them."

"Hmm. If you wait until after practice, I can join you," Keisha suggested. "I could hit Gold-Karat Jewelers and see if the earring gives me a lead."

"Good call," Carlos said.

They reached the top of the steps. The twins split off for class, and Keisha and Carlos continued on their way. "So, any thoughts about the Spirit Squad case?" Carlos asked.

Keisha shrugged. "I don't know. Aside from the random clues, I've got no suspects. Plus, Frankie and I had a fight. Again. I'm not sure what to think."

Just then, a familiar voice beside them said, "Hello, Keisha."

She turned to see Nadia approaching. The blonde girl had the same rigid posture as she did at practice. She clutched her textbooks close to her chest.

"Hey, Nadia," Keisha said.

"I hear Frankie's injury is not severe, though she is using a crutch," Nadia said.

"Yeah, I guess so," Keisha replied.

"Good. I am glad she's doing well," Nadia said. Then added, "Coach has made me captain now that Frankie is out of commission."

Keisha was about to respond when she looked at the books in Nadia's arms. A flicker of recognition lit a wildfire in her mind. At the front of the stack was an issue of *Cheer For Today* magazine. It wasn't the first time she'd seen Nadia reading the mag, but it was the first time she noticed the cover.

Specifically, she noticed the F in the word For. It was big, bold, and glittering pink.

It's just like the one in the 'Frankie Beware' note! Keisha thought.

"I'll see you at practice," Keisha told Nadia.

As Nadia walked down the hall, Carlos noticed the look on Keisha's face. "I know that look," he said. "You just figured something out, right?"

"Sure did," Keisha said. "I think I just found my first suspect."

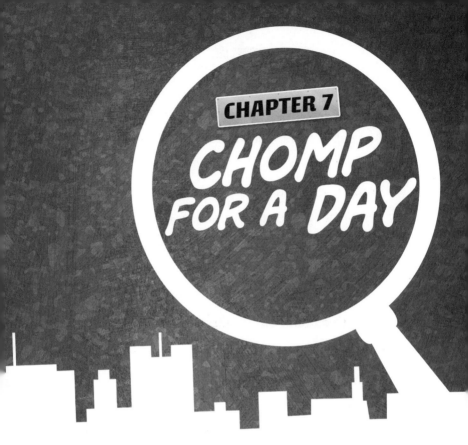

CHAPTER 7

CHOMP
FOR A DAY

Keisha arrived at practice ready to keep an eye on Nadia. Whoever had cut out the note for Frankie had used a copy of *Cheer For Today*, and Keisha had seen the new girl reading the magazine on more than one occasion. During the school day, Keisha tried to learn more info on Nadia. She hadn't found much, but she did learn that Nadia liked to take charge, to be a leader.

But would she purposely injure Frankie to take over as captain? Keisha wondered as she entered the gym.

Frankie was seated on the bleachers. A crutch lay across her lap, and her injured ankle was wrapped. She pretended not to notice Keisha.

"Bring it in, girls," Coach Buchanan said, gathering the girls around her. "Before we begin, we need to change our lineup after yesterday's accident." She looked over at Frankie. "Nadia will be our new captain, and Iris will have to take Frankie's spot. That means our new girl, Keisha —"

Keisha had been thinking about the case and not paying attention. "Huh?" she blurted out.

"You're going to be our new Chomp. Congratulations," Coach Buchanan said.

"Wait. I'm the new what?"

Keisha stood dumbfounded as Iris held out the Chomp costume.

Keisha shot Frankie a look that said, *This was NOT part of the deal.* Then she snatched the costume from Iris. "Fine," she said.

Keisha struggled into the bulky costume. It was heavy and smelled like sweat. She gagged as she pulled the straps over her shoulders, and immediately dreaded having to place the head on.

"Looks like this is all yours now," Iris said, wielding the T-shirt cannon. Iris handled the device easily, and she looked way too happy to give up her role as Chomp. Keisha suddenly wondered if Iris was the culprit behind Frankie's injury. She did have access to the T-shirt cannon, after all.

Her suspect list had just doubled.

"Okay, squad!" Coach Buchanan clapped loudly. "Let's go!"

It was bad enough learning to walk in the heavy, bulky suit. But Coach Buchanan expected her to dance in it.

An hour later, the squad took a break. Keisha strained to remove the giant mascot head. When it was off, she gulped the cool air of the gym like she'd just surfaced from underwater.

"Everything okay?" Coach Buchanan asked.

Keisha nodded.

"Don't worry," Iris said, smiling and patting her on the shoulder. "You're doin' a great job." She and Amelia Thornton giggled and jogged over to a water fountain to refill their bottles.

As Keisha waddled over to sit, she heard a voice behind her whisper, "Shh! We can't talk about it here. What if Frankie overhears?"

"Fine," a second voice hissed. "But when?"

"After practice."

Keisha casually turned, acting like she hadn't heard the voices. Nearby, Kate and Stella stood together, heads nearly pressed against one another.

Well, that's suspicious, Keisha thought. Two more suspects had suddenly been added to her list.

Keisha had time to catch a quick drink from her water bottle before Coach Buchanan shouted, "Back in line! Let's do it again!"

The girls took their places and waited for the music to begin. Keisha hefted the bulldog head back on; it immediately felt like she'd been dropped into a sauna again.

As she paraded around in front of the team, Keisha's mind drifted to the mystery at hand. She'd arrived at practice with one suspect in mind: Nadia. But suddenly, several others had appeared.

So who had left the note? And who fired the T-shirt cannon?

Was it Nadia and her desire to be the Spirit Squad captain? Or would Iris do anything to get out of the stifling Chomp costume? Or could it be Stella and Kate, whose secret conversation apparently had something to do with Frankie?

Keisha was so distracted by her thoughts that she forgot where she was in the routine. She stepped back and caught the right paw of her costume on the edge of the blue mat. She stumbled, waving her arms wildly.

"Whoa!" She crashed into the Spirit Squad's shaky human pyramid. The girls screamed and fell to the mat in a heaping mass of flailing limbs. Keisha tripped over a fallen Amelia and landed hard on her back. Chomp's head sailed off, rolling across the gym floor like it had been decapitated.

"Ouch," Keisha said quietly as others moaned and groaned.

"Nice work," Stella said.

"Really graceful," Kate added.

"Is everyone okay?" Coach Buchanan rushed over to help. She pulled Keisha off the floor; the junior detective wobbled, then righted herself.

Because of the blue mats, no one was seriously hurt, just bruised and battered. But they were still angry.

"Coach," Stella said, "There's no way we're gonna win Cheer Bonanza with Miss Clumsy there as our Chomp."

"Yeah," Kate said. "We're doomed."

Keisha stood there, embarrassed, as everyone complained about her. Incompetent. Weak. Klutzy. These names, and worse, were tossed out. She looked at Frankie, hoping her old friend would defend her. But Frankie just stared at her crutch.

Keisha's embarrassment turned to anger. She couldn't take it anymore. "Fine!" she shouted, tugging down the Chomp costume and climbing out of it. "You win! I don't have to take this from a bunch of spoiled brats."

Keisha stormed across the gym. As she passed the Chomp head, she kicked it hard. It skittered across the floor toward the stunned, suddenly quiet crowd of girls.

Keisha left the gym without looking back.

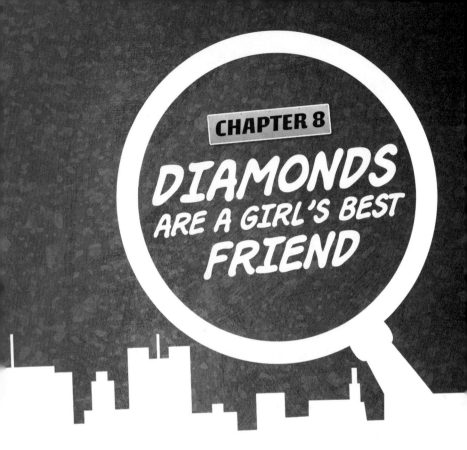

CHAPTER 8

DIAMONDS ARE A GIRL'S BEST FRIEND

"Here, maybe this Raspberry 'Ruption will calm you down."

Jaden passed the extra-large juice drink to Keisha. She took it grudgingly and sipped. He was right. It did help, a little. But she was still stewing about what had happened at Spirit Squad practice.

Keisha and the other Snoops were walking through the Burlington Mall food court after making a pit stop at Juicy Smoothius. The scent of hamburgers, pizza, and cinnamon rolls filled the air around them.

The two-story mall was wedged onto a single city block, right on the 'El' line and a quick ride from the Snoops' apartment building.

"Gold-Karat Jewelers is on the west side," Keisha said, pointing. "Where all the uppity, ritzy stores are located."

"And the arcade is that way." Carlos nodded in the opposite direction.

"You're still cool with solving this case?" Hayden asked. "Even after what happened today?"

Keisha shrugged. "Snoops, Inc. has never quit a case yet. No point in starting now."

"Right on," Carlos said. He checked his watch. "We've got some time before our meeting at the arcade. Let's hit the jewelry store first."

Keisha and her parents never shopped on the mall's west side. The stores there were the kind that sold T-shirts for a hundred bucks apiece. She felt awkward being there and made a beeline for Gold-Karat Jewelers.

The store seemed to gleam as brightly as the jewels it sold. The gold display cases were filled with gems, rings, and necklaces with incredibly high price tags.

An older man, tall and thin and wearing a brown tweed suit coat, stood behind the counter. He had a long face and perfectly combed gray hair.

"May I assist you?" he asked, sounding like he already knew the answer was no.

Hayden withdrew the plastic bag containing the diamond earring from her backpack and handed it to Keisha.

Keisha slid it onto the glass counter in front of the man. "Do you sell this earring here?"

The jeweler stared down his nose at Keisha. He picked up the bag and glanced at it. "This appears to be a Francois Guion," he said, confirming Frankie's initial guess. "We are, of course, the only sellers of said jewelry in the city."

He reached into his pocket and removed a small, circular black lens. Placing it on his left eye, he squinted and peered closer at the earring.

"Hmmmm," he finally said. "It is a fake."

"What?" Keisha was baffled.

"A fake," the man repeated. "This is not a diamond at all, but a cubic zirconia. The setting is a close match to a Guion, but it is not the same."

"So this earring is worth . . ." Keisha prodded.

"Less than fifty dollars," the man said.

He slid the bag back to Keisha.

"Huh. Thanks," Keisha said. She took the bag and they quickly exited the jewelry store.

"I don't get it," Jaden said. "So it's not real?"

"Not expensive or unique," Hayden said.

"Which sounds like the kind of thing a Spirit Squad girl would avoid wearing at all costs," Keisha said.

"Unless they're only pretending to be rich," Carlos said. "Because they don't want anyone to find out they're not."

Keisha pocketed the bag. The pieces of the mystery seemed to be flying around her, swirling and twirling and not letting her grasp them.

"Time to head to Al's Castle," Carlos informed the others.

The quartet walked toward the arcade. As they did, Keisha spied two girls heading in their direction. Her heart skipped a beat.

Keisha grabbed Jaden's arm and pulled him behind a large potted plant. Carlos and Hayden followed. "Act casual," she whispered.

"Casual?" Jaden whispered back roughly. "Like 'duck and hide' casual?"

The two girls passed the hidden Snoops unaware. It was Stella Lyndon and Kate Nicholson. They were both looking down at their phones, texting and walking.

"I'm gonna follow them," Keisha said.

"But we've got the arcade case," Carlos said.

"Go solve it then." Keisha began to slink off behind the girls, leaving the other Snoops behind.

She glanced back and watched her friends head toward the arcade while she moved in the opposite direction. That was basically how this whole mystery had felt for her. She wasn't getting any guidance from Carlos, no tech savvy from Hayden, and no random jokes from Jaden.

She felt completely on her own.

Ahead of her, Stella and Kate entered a clothing store named Always 18. Keisha followed, but not too close.

The store's music was loud and distracting. Keisha saw the duo near the back, checking out a rack of dresses. She slipped closer until the only thing between her and the Spirit Squaders was a circular rack of colorful shirts.

"Cheer Bonanza is going to be so . . ." Keisha heard Kate say.

"I can't believe Frankie . . ." Stella was saying.

The loud music made it hard to hear the girls. *But they're talking about Frankie*, Keisha thought. *They could admit their guilt right here and now.*

She needed to get closer.

Keisha slipped into the middle of the clothes rack. She crouched, hidden from view, listening as she fumbled for her phone. If Keisha wanted to blow this case wide open, she needed to record the audio for proof.

"Speaking of Frankie," Kate began, "There's no way we're gonna invite her, are we?"

"Nuh-uh," Stella said. "Especially not since she's hanging out with that Turner girl again. What was Frankie thinking, bringing her onto the Spirit Squad?"

Wait. What?

"If we're signing the Spirit Squad up for summer cheer camp, I do not want Frankie to find out," Kate said.

"That's what I was going to say at practice today," Stella explained. "Before you shut me up."

So that's what they were talking about? Summer cheer camp? They weren't behind the threats against Frankie. The two girls just simply didn't like her. Keisha scowled and clicked off her phone in frustration.

"If Frankie finds out we're signing up, she'll probably try to invite that loser detective friend of hers," Stella said.

"O-M-G, did you see the look on her face when she ruined our 'cheer-amid' today?" Kate asked.

The two girls began to laugh.

Keisha's ears burned. She had to get away — fast. She angrily brushed aside the clothes and ducked out of the rack the way she'd entered it.

Or at least, she tried to. Her foot caught on the rack's bottom rail. It slid sideways and struck a display of mannequins, knocking them over like dominoes. The last mannequin landed next to a young boy shopping with his mother. The boy let out a terrified scream.

For the second time that day, Keisha had caused a gigantic scene.

She lay on the floor surrounded by fallen clothing and mannequins. She stared up at the ceiling as a confused Kate and Stella walked over and stared down at her.

"Hey," Keisha said. "Find anything on sale?"

CHAPTER 9

ON THE RIGHT TRACK

The two Spirit Squad girls were stunned silent. Keisha stood and brushed herself off.

"What's going on here?" a panicked female employee asked as she surveyed the damage. The mother of the small boy, who was still bawling, dragged him away from the mannequin carnage.

Keisha glanced at Stella and Kate. The two were snickering at her.

"Uh . . . sorry," she said, standing and heading for the exit.

"Hey!" an employee called out, but Keisha didn't stop. She raced out of the store and tore through the mall. She found the other Snoops standing outside Al's Castle Arcade. The owner, Al, was shaking Carlos's hand.

"Thank you so much, Snoops, Incorporated," he said, heading back into the arcade.

"Hey, Keisha!" Carlos said happily when he saw her. "We solved the case!"

"Carlos was right," Hayden said. "It was Al's new employee."

"He tried to run away when we busted him," Carlos said.

"So I lobbed a skee-ball at him," Jaden said proudly, before adding, "I missed."

"But he did hit the *Meteorites* machine," Hayden said. "It scared the kid so much, he tripped and fell into a ball pit."

"Wow," Keisha said. "Sounds eventful." It felt weird, missing out on solving a case with the crew. This was the first time she hadn't been there to help wrap things up. It bummed her out, like she was choosing between the Snoops and Frankie all over again.

"Al's giving us a bucket of tokens as payment," Jaden said. "You wanna play some air hockey?"

Keisha shook her head. "Nah," she said. "I think I'm gonna call it a night. Sorry."

"Okay," Carlos said. Keisha could tell he knew something was up, but Carlos knew better than to push it.

So while the rest of the team headed into the loud arcade, Keisha left and headed home.

* * *

Hands in her pockets, a glum Keisha walked down the darkened sidewalk through pools of streetlights. As she reached an intersection, the 'El' train rattled above her. She looked up as the train passed and felt the CTA pass she had found at school in her pocket. She walked to the nearest set of steps leading to a train platform.

The platform wasn't crowded. A man played saxophone while people tossed loose change into his case. Keisha read the lit up sign hanging off a beam; the next train toward home would arrive in ten minutes.

But then a train going the opposite direction arrived. For some reason, Keisha decided to use the 'El' pass and climbed aboard that train instead.

She found a seat by the window and leaned her forehead against the glass. Keisha didn't want to think about Frankie and The Fallout. But she couldn't help it. She hated Frankie's actions. Making her choose between her friends, and the results of that choice — it all still hurt as much as when it first happened. Keisha brushed back tears and watched the skyline buzz by in a blur.

She was staring out the window when a building caught her attention. Her energy suddenly returned. When the 'El' train hissed to a stop, Keisha leaped off and hurried down to the street below.

The neighborhood was old and abandoned. Many storefronts were shuttered or empty. The building Keisha had seen was mostly surrounded by chain-link fence. Residents could still access it, but work had already begun around it.

Keisha craned her neck up at the building's sign. "Kent Tower," she read. Below the sign hung a banner with the words:

FUTURE HOME OF DIXON DENTAL ORTHODONTIC CENTER.

As Keisha approached the building, she scanned the construction area. Mounds of gravel and red clay dirt were heaped near the fence; some of it spilled out onto the sidewalk.

"This looks a lot like the dirt and gravel in Dr. Dixon's office," she whispered to herself.

She climbed the small set of cracked steps. Taped to the front door was a notice of eviction.

The residents of Kent Tower are being kicked out so Frankie's dad can tear the building down, she thought.

Next to the door was an intercom system used for buzzing in guests. It had two rows of buttons.

Names written on small scraps of paper were taped beside each button.

Keisha examined the list of names.

"Bingo," she whispered to herself.

One of the names was familiar. The pieces of the puzzle suddenly came together. Everything was starting to make sense. She wanted to gather the Snoops and tell them she'd done it.

But there was someplace she had to go first.

Fifteen minutes later, Keisha was riding up the glass elevator at Frankie's building. When the door slid open, Frankie stood there leaning on her crutch. She didn't look very happy to see Keisha.

"What is it now?" Frankie asked, irritated.

"I need you to do something for me."

Frankie was surprised. "Really? What's that?"

"Just promise me you'll do it," Keisha urged. "I'll be Chomp in the Cheer Bonanza, and I won't complain about it. All right?"

"Why would you do that?"

"Because I know who knocked you out of the competition."

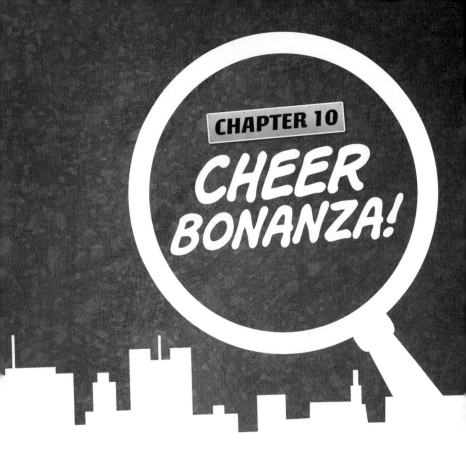

CHAPTER 10

CHEER BONANZA!

"Aaannnd welcome to the regional Cheer Bonanza!" the voice on the loudspeaker blared. The packed bleachers in the Fleischman Middle School gymnasium roared with excitement. Colorful banners hung in the halls. The cafeteria had been turned into a waiting area for the competing teams. Cheer squads from a dozen schools practiced their routines wherever they could find space.

Keisha stood in amazement at the gym door as the team from Fleischman's rivals, the Watson Hurricanes, performed their routine. Loud music echoed off the walls.

"Better hurry up," Frankie said from behind her. "You're up next."

Despite still relying on a crutch to get around, Frankie was dressed in her Spirit Squad uniform. It had been a few days since Keisha had solved the mystery and rejoined the team. She and Frankie had decided to wait until after the Cheer Bonanza to confront the culprit. They didn't want to jeopardize their chances of winning anymore than they already had.

It had only taken a brief talk with Coach Buchanan to get Keisha back on the squad. Frankie had been right; they needed her.

Keisha and Frankie hadn't spoken about their most recent argument. They just pretended that it hadn't happened, and that the small mending they'd done to their friendship before the recent argument was still in place.

Earlier that day Keisha had run the case and her conclusions by the other Snoops. They had all agreed that she had cracked the case. Carlos told her, "Brilliant! I knew you'd figure it out."

Now when Keisha looked up in the stands she saw Carlos, Hayden, and Jaden seated together. They saw her and waved. She was glad her friends were there to support her.

Coach Buchanan had the Spirit Squad huddle together outside the gymnasium. As Keisha and Frankie joined the group, Keisha stole a quick glance at the culprit.

"All right," Coach Buchanan said, "this is what you've been training for. So go out there and show those judges what a champion looks like!"

The girls whooped and hollered.

Keisha got into the Chomp costume, which smelled as bad as ever.

"And now," the announcer said as Keisha dropped the bulldog's head into place, "here to represent Fleischman Middle School, it's the Fleischman Spirit Squad!"

Keisha led the way into the gym, waving her arms at the crowd. The girls lined up in staggered rows, heads down, until the music began. Then they came to life. Keisha, under the mascot head, couldn't see the action, but she knew the girls were moving fluidly across the gym. Amelia's series of back handsprings in front of the group wowed the crowd.

As the music wrapped up, Keisha took her cue and slipped to the rear of the squad where the T-shirt cannon was propped up on a stand. She grabbed it, and as the music and routine ended, she pulled the trigger.

WHOOMP!

Confetti rained down on the Spirit Squad, filling the gymnasium. The crowd loved it. Their cheering rang out across the gym.

"That was amazing!" Nadia said as they jogged out of the gym. Her normal no-nonsense front was gone; a wide smile stretched across her face. The group shared hugs and high-fives. Frankie joined in the celebration.

"Great job, everyone." Coach Buchanan beamed proudly. "You really stepped up, Chomp."

"Thanks, Coach," Keisha said. A couple girls offered their thanks as well. Keisha noticed that Stella and Kate, who hadn't spoken of their run-in at Always 18, were not among them.

"Let's go watch the competition," Coach Buchanan said. The girls eagerly filed back into the gym. Keisha, still in her Chomp costume, wanted to change into her outfit. But she needed help.

"Hey Amelia," she said, tapping the girl on her shoulder, "Got a sec?"

Amelia, with her gold star earrings glimmering in the light, stopped. "Sure," she said.

Keisha began to unzip the Chomp costume. Her Spirit Squad outfit underneath was soaked with sweat. She waited until the last of the team had entered the gym before telling Amelia, "I think I have your 'El' pass."

Amelia froze, briefly. It was just a flicker of hesitation. "Have you been on the 'El'?" she asked. "It's disgusting. I wouldn't be caught dead on it."

"Cut the act," Keisha said, not angrily. "I know you ruined the Dixon Dental model and left the threatening note for Frankie. And I know you fired the T-shirt cannon at us."

"No I didn't." She said it without conviction.

"It's okay," Keisha said. "I get it. These girls, this squad . . . you have a reputation. So you pretend not to ride the 'El' and you wear fake Francois Guion earrings. And you don't tell a single soul that Frankie's dad is kicking your family out of your home."

Tears were forming in Amelia's eyes.

"I rode the train to Kent Tower the other night," Keisha said. "I saw the name Thornton on the building's directory. You live there, right?"

"Don't tell the girls," Amelia said.

"You think they'll care where you live? How rich, or how poor, you are?" Keisha asked gently.

"Yes! They'll make fun of me."

"Then make them see they're wrong," Keisha said. "Show them that money doesn't define a person's worth. Rise above all that."

Keisha had finished taking off the Chomp outfit.

"Look," she said. "It's not my place to tell the girls. And certainly not here. Enjoy the moment. But I had to tell Frankie, and I made her swear her secrecy . . . and to one other thing."

Amelia was chewing her bottom lip. She perked up at this. "What?" she asked.

"Dr. Dixon has put the project on hold," Keisha said. "To give Kent Tower residents time to find someplace nice to live."

There was a long, silent pause. Amelia stared at the floor and quietly said, "Thank you." She paused again, then continued. "It was a dumb thing to do. I was just so mad. I cut up one of my old issues of *Cheer For Today* and smashed the model. I didn't realize one of my earrings was missing until the next day. Then when I saw you and Frankie practicing alone, I tried to scare you with the confetti. I didn't think Frankie would fall so hard. I really didn't want anyone to get hurt."

The crowd in the gym cheered again as the announcer presented the next squad.

Carlos' head popped out of the gym door. "Hey! There you are. Everything cool?"

She looked over at Amelia, who was drying her eyes with one sleeve. Amelia nodded.

"I think so," Keisha said.

"I'm so sorry," Amelia said.

"All good." Keisha slipped an arm over Amelia's shoulder. "You really need to have a chat with Frankie, though."

Together, they walked into the raucous gym, where they joined the rest of the team in the bleachers. The Snoops were with them. Jaden doted on Frankie, making sure she was okay and constantly asking if she needed anything.

When the final performance was finished, the teams gathered on the gym floor. Each squad stood in a tight circle, holding hands and lowering their heads in anticipation. Fleischman's principal, Mr. Snider, walked over and took over the microphone.

"What a marvelous competition today!" he boomed. "Great work, teams. Now, the third place winner is . . . Youngstown Middle School!"

The team from Youngstown, dressed in pink and white, leaped to their feet.

"In second place . . ." Principal Snider consulted the slip of paper in his hand. "Our very own Fleischman Spirit Squad!"

Keisha and the girls hugged and congratulated one another as someone passed them the silver second place trophy. Keisha had to admit that she was a little bummed they hadn't won. Still, considering everything that had happened in the last few days, second place was remarkably good.

The first place trophy went to Watson Middle School. *Of course*, Keisha thought. The Bulldogs' rival accepted their trophy, which they lifted high into the air.

"Congratulations, Chomp," Frankie said, walking over with the other Snoops.

"Ready to rejoin the team?" Keisha asked. "'Cuz I can't be a giant bulldog anymore."

"I don't know," Frankie pondered. "Maybe I should join Snoops, Incorporated on their next case. Solving a mystery might be fun."

Jaden's eyes grew wide, and it looked like his heart was about to explode with confetti.

Keisha couldn't believe her ears. "It ain't all glitz and glamour, Frankie," she said. "Sometimes you have to hang out in a dumpster with Jaden."

"A what?!" Frankie shook her head. "Ugh. I take it back. I'll stick to Spirit Squad and leave solving crimes to my new ex-BFF."

THE END

Snoops, Inc. Case Report #006

Prepared by Keisha Turner

THE CASE:
Find out which of the Spirit Squad girls left an ominous note saying 'FRANKIE BEWARE' and ruined the building model of Dr. Dixon's new dental clinic.

CRACKING THE CASE:
I get it. Frankie Dixon can be a real pain. We used to be close friends, but that changed when she, well, when The Fallout happened. Anyway, while the other Snoops were working another case, I went undercover as the newest member of the Spirit Squad to try to find the culprit.

Going undercover can stink sometimes, literally. Like when Jaden and I staked out an alley to catch a jewelry thief. The only place to hide was in a smelly dumpster. How could we see anything from inside a dumpster? Glad you asked.

We made a tiny hole and created a pinhole camera. Hayden showed me how it works. Basically, a pinhole camera, or a 'camera obscura,' is a very small hole in a dark place that acts like a lens. It focuses the light and creates an upside-down image at a certain point. But don't ask me to explain any more than that. It makes my brain hurt.

The pinhole camera didn't help solve Frankie's Spirit Squad case. But when it came to Barney Marsh, it definitely helped us to . . .

CRACK THE CASE! ▮

WHAT DO YOU THINK?

1. The Spirit Squad is a group who shows school pride at Fleischman Middle School. Are you a member of any school groups? What kind of activities do the groups do?

2. Keisha continues to investigate Frankie's case even after the girls have a fight. Why doesn't she quit? What motivates Keisha to keep going with the investigation?

3. Amelia Thornton fears the Spirit Squad girls will not accept her if they find out where she lives. Why is this? Give some examples of how Amelia pretends to be just like the other girls.

WRITE YOUR OWN!

1. Keisha feels lonely since she isn't working with the Snoops and doesn't fit in with the Spirit Squad. Have you ever felt this way? Write a diary entry to explain how you felt.

2. Keisha and Frankie enjoy remembering the fun times they had as best friends. Write about a special time you spent having fun with a friend or loved one.

3. Frankie is injured right before the big Cheer Bonanza. Have you ever missed out on a special event you looked forward to? Write about your experience.

GLOSSARY

CULPRIT (KUHL-prit)—someone who is guilty of doing something wrong or of committing a crime

'EL' TRAIN (EL TRAYN)—a train set on elevated tracks that run over city streets

EVICTION (ih-VICK-shuhn)—to be legally expelled from a building, usually for nonpayment of rent

EVIDENCE (EV-uh-duhnss)—information, items, and facts that help prove something to be true or false

MANNEQUIN (MAN-ih-kin)—a life-sized dummy used to display clothing

RESIDENT (REZ-ih-duhnt)—a person who lives in a place

ROUTINE (roo-TEEN)—a set of tasks done in a set order

STAKEOUT (STAKE-out)—a situation in which someone watches a place to look for suspicious activity

SUITE (SWEET)—a series of connected rooms in a hotel or apartment building

ABOUT THE AUTHOR

Brandon Terrell has been a lifelong fan of mysteries, shown by his collection of nearly 200 Hardy Boys books. He is the author of numerous children's books, including several titles in series such as Tony Hawk's 900 Revolution, Jake Maddox Graphic Novels, Spine Shivers, and Sports Illustrated Kids: Time Machine Magazine.

When not hunched over his laptop, Brandon enjoys watching movies and television, reading, watching and playing baseball, and spending time at home with his wife and two children in Minnesota.

ABOUT THE ILLUSTRATOR

Mariano Epelbaum is an experienced character designer, illustrator, and traditional 2D animator. He has been working as a professional artist since 1996 and enjoys trying different art styles and techniques.

Throughout his career Mariano has created many expressive characters and designs for a wide range of films, TV series, commercials, and publications in his native country of Argentina. In addition to Snoops, Inc., Mariano has also contributed to the Fairy Tale Mixups and You Choose: Fractured Fairy Tales series for Capstone.

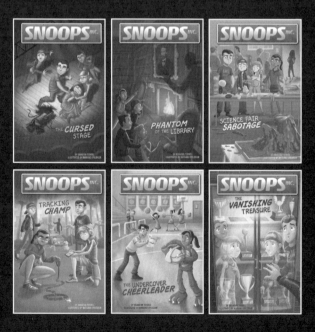